This book belongs to:

_____

THE
OCTOPUS
WAY

WRITTEN BY TINA LAVALLEE

ILLUSTRATED BY AMANDA PECHOUSEK

To Cale & Chloe, my inspirations, for the infinite smiles,
love and laughter. Never stop dreaming.
- Kisses, Aunty T

To Adrian & Owen, may your curiosity and sense of wonder be as
boundless as my love for you.
- Love, Mommy

Written by Tina Lavallee
Illustrated by Amanda Pechousek
ISBN: 978-1-7387480-4-4 (Paperback) | ISBN: 978-1-7387480-2-0 (Hardcover)
ISBN: 978-1-7387480-0-6 (Boardbook) | ISBN: 978-1-7387480-1-3 (eBook)
ISBN: 978-1-7387480-3-7 (Audio)

First edition April 2023.

For information, contact us at:
www.caleandchloe.com

A WORLD TO DISCOVER,
EACH DAY A NEW WAY.
THE MYSTERIES OF NATURE,
WHAT WILL WE BE TODAY?

CALE & CHLOE

A New Day, A New Way
Series

What will we be today?
What facts will we convey?

Today is OCTOPUS day.
Hooray, hooray, hooray!

Chloe, look...

We can squeeze through anything,
we have absolutely no bones.

And these are our dens,
we each get our own.

I guess they're not social,
and prefer to sleep alone.

We have three hearts,
and our blood is blue.

And Cale,
we can see better than most people do.

Our limbs are called arms,
not tentacles like some say.

And they're not always long,
not arcticus' anyway.

BATHYPOLYPUS ARCTICUS

Over three hundred species,
and one of the smartest.

The octopus history,
is one of the longest.

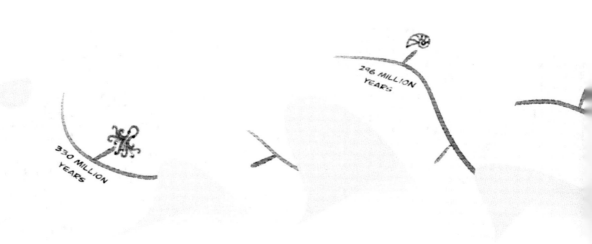

330 MILLION
YEARS

296 MILLION
YEARS

TODAY

95 MILLION
YEARS

Wolfi's the smallest,
Pacific's the largest.

And vulgaris, by far,
is the coolest, the sharpest.

We are tricky to spot,
with our ability to blend.

We need this advantage.
Sadly, not everyone's our friend.

Eight arms, with eight brains,
each act on their own.

Open jars, solve puzzles,
even talk on the phone.

They feel, taste, and smell,
and so much more than is known.

Now that we've learned
The Octopus Way,
Cale and Chloe,
the night's on its way.

It's time to get rest,
until our next quest.
Tomorrow's a new day,
and we'll learn a new way.

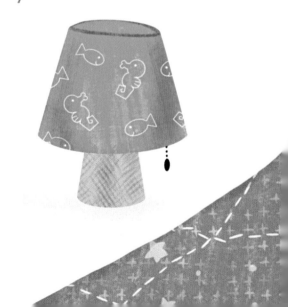

Manufactured by Amazon.ca
Bolton, ON

34154022R00017